W 12.95

☑ S0-BJM-062

MARY A. WHITE SCHOOL
Library Media Center
Grand Haven, MI 49417

ALISON RIDES THE RAPIDS
by Nina Alexander

Illustrations by
Gabriel Picart

Spot Illustrations by
Rich Grote

MAGIC ATTIC PRESS

Published by Magic Attic Press.

Copyright ©1998 by MAGIC ATTIC PRESS

All rights reserved. No part of this book
may be used or reproduced in any manner whatsoever
without written permission except in the case of a
brief quotation embodied in critical articles and reviews.

For more information contact:
Book Editor, Magic Attic Press, 866 Spring Street,
Westbrook, ME 04092-3808

First Edition
Printed in the United States of America
1 2 3 4 5 6 7 8 9 10

Magic Attic Club® is a registered trademark.

Betsy Gould, Publisher
Marva Martin, Art Director
Jay Brady, Managing Editor

Edited by Judit Bodnar
Designed by Cindy Vacek

Alexander, Nina
Alison Rides the Rapids / by Nina Alexander:
illustrations by Gabriel Picart, spot illustrations by Rich Grote
(Magic Attic Club)
Summary: Alison is always up for a good adventure. She finds herself in training as a
Junior River Guide on a whitewater rafting trip. But when the Senior Guide falls
overboard, how will Alison rescue her and make sure the others are safe?
ISBN 1-57513-122-6 (hardback) ISBN 1-57513-121-8 (paperback)
ISBN 1-57513-141-2 (library edition hardback)

Lbrary of Congress Cataloging in Publication Data is on file at the Library of Congress

As members of the
MAGIC ATTIC CLUB,
we promise to
be best friends,
share all of our adventures in the attic,
use our imaginations,
have lots of fun together,
and remember—the real magic is in us.

Alison   Keisha

Heather   Megan

Rose

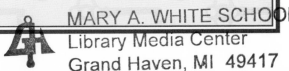

MARY A. WHITE SCHOOL
Library Media Center
Grand Haven, MI 49417

Table of Contents

Prologue

When Alison, Heather, Keisha, and Megan find a golden key buried in the snow, they have no idea that it will change their lives forever. They discover that it belongs to Ellie Goodwin, the owner of an old Victorian house across the street from Alison's. Ellie, grateful when they return the key to her, invites the girls to play in her attic. There they find a steamer trunk filled with wonderful outfits—party dresses, a princess gown, a ballet tutu, cowgirl clothes, and many, many, more. The girls try on some of the costumes and admire their reflections in a tall, gilded mirror nearby. Suddenly they are transported to a new time and place, embarking on the greatest adventure of their lives.

After they return to the present and Ellie's attic, they form the Magic Attic Club, promising to tell each other every exciting detail of their future adventures. Then they meet Rose Hopkins, a new girl at school, and invite her to join the club and share their amazing secret.

Chapter
One

THE SUBSTITUTE TEACHER

Alison McCann tapped her pencil on her desk. She twisted a strand of her long blond hair around her finger and wriggled her feet back and forth. Then she sighed and looked at her watch.

School had only started an hour before, but Alison couldn't wait to get outside. It was a crisp autumn day, and she would much rather have been playing kickball or hanging out with her friends than sitting in math class. She glanced at the teacher at the front of the room.

Her regular fifth-grade teacher, Ms. Austin, was out sick, and a substitute was teaching the class. His name was Mr. Hartley. He was a tall, thin young man with wavy brown hair and wire-rimmed glasses. He had never taught the class before. Alison thought he seemed nice.

Still, she was having a hard time following the math lesson he was teaching. It wasn't because it was too hard— Alison was smart, and she usually did quite well in her classes. But today she felt restless. She kept thinking about all the interesting things she could be doing outside.

Alison glanced over at her friend Megan Ryder, who was sitting several aisles away. Megan was paying close attention as Mr. Hartley explained the word problem he had written on the blackboard.

Alison sighed again. Megan always paid attention in class. Alison wondered how she did it. School could be so boring sometimes—especially when the teacher was talking about word problems.

"All right, class," Mr. Hartley said a few minutes later. "Put your books away. Time for a surprise test!"

"Uh-oh," Alison whispered to herself. She wished she had paid closer attention to the lesson. But it was too late now.

The teacher walked up and down the aisles, placing a copy of the test on each desk. Alison felt more nervous than ever. The test consisted of several pages stapled together, with lots of typing on each page. Flipping through, she counted ten word problems. Her heart sank. With her learning disability, it would take her forever to get through them all!

Having dyslexia meant that Alison had more trouble reading than most people did. Certain letters and words got switched around in her head, and she had to concentrate to understand things that her friends could read with ease. Thanks to the special tutor her parents had hired, she was getting a lot better at reading. But long assignments with lots and lots of words still made her nervous.

Ms. Austin and Alison's other regular teachers knew about her dyslexia, but Mr. Hartley didn't. He had no idea how much scarier and harder this long test would be for her than for the rest of the class.

Alison stared at the top sheet. The first problem was five lines long. She felt tears sting her eyes, but she shook them away angrily. She wasn't going to let a few stupid questions on a quiz beat her.

She picked up her pencil, took a deep breath, and started to read.

"Okay, time's up," Mr. Hartley announced half an hour later.

Alison couldn't believe it.

She was only on the sixth problem! Still, there wasn't much she could do about it. The test was over. She quickly scribbled a few guesses down for the remaining questions, then passed her paper forward.

Alison dragged her feet as she left the room to go to lunch. Her four best friends were waiting for her in the hallway.

Alison, Megan, and Keisha Vance had been friends for years. More recently, Heather Hardin and Rose Hopkins had joined their group. Besides being best friends, the five girls had another important connection. They all knew the secret of the very special attic of their friend Ellie Goodwin's house. Ellie, who lived across the street from Alison's family, had once been a professional actress and singer. These days she taught music, dance, and acting in her home. Her old Victorian house was full of all kinds of surprises, and none was more surprising than her attic. Whenever any of the girls put on one of the exotic outfits she found there and looked into the gilded full-length mirror, she was instantly transported to another time and place. After their first exciting adventure, the girls had formed the Magic Attic Club.

Right now, Alison wasn't thinking about Ellie or her incredible attic. She was still thinking about the math test. She knew she hadn't done very well on it. She had been so busy trying to rush through all the problems that she wasn't sure about some of the answers she had written down.

"That test was kind of fun, wasn't it?" said Heather, pushing back her dark hair.

Keisha nodded. "I like Mr. Hartley, and his word problems were funny. It made the whole test seem easier."

Alison frowned. She hadn't really noticed anything humorous about the test! "Come on," she said. She didn't feel like talking about the test anymore, even with her best friends. "Let's get to lunch. I'm starving."

By the time the lunch period ended, Alison had almost forgotten about the math test. She and her friends had talked about other things while they ate—sports, their upcoming choir concert, Keisha's latest adventure in Ellie's attic. Alison was in a much better mood when she got back to Ms. Austin's classroom.

But when she saw Mr. Hartley standing at the front of the room holding a stack of papers, her heart sank. It looked like all the papers had already been corrected. She dreaded seeing her grade.

"Welcome back, class,"

Mr. Hartley began. "I hope you all had a nice lunch. I know I did. I spent my lunch period in the teacher's lounge correcting your test papers. And I'm happy to say that most of you did very well."

Not me, Alison thought glumly. She sank lower in her seat as Mr. Hartley began calling names.

It seemed to take the teacher forever to get to Alison's paper. Finally he called her name. Alison jumped out of her chair and hurried to the front of the room, not meeting his eyes as she took the paper from his hand.

She folded it over quickly without looking at it. She

wanted to get back to her seat and sit down before she checked her grade.

At her desk, Alison took a deep breath, then closed her eyes and unfolded the test paper. Crossing her fingers, she opened her eyes and looked down.

She stared at the paper in horror. At the top of the first page, written in bright red ink, was 35%.

It was even worse than she had feared.

She had flunked the test!

Chapter

TWO

MR. HARTLEY'S OFFER

O h, no!" Alison whispered. She kept staring at the bright red number in front of her, hoping it would suddenly change to a passing grade. What were her parents going to say when they saw it? What was she going to do? This could lower her whole grade for the year!

Suddenly she realized that someone was calling her name. "Alison," Mr. Hartley said loudly. "Earth to Alison!"

"Huh?" Alison glanced up. The teacher was standing in

front of her. "Uh, sorry," she said sheepishly. "What did you say?"

Mr. Hartley smiled gently at her. His gray eyes looked kind and concerned. "I was wondering if you could stay behind and talk to me for a few minutes at the end of the day," he said.

"Sure," Alison said nervously.

The teacher smiled again, then turned and headed to the blackboard to start the next lesson.

Alison slumped in her seat and stared ahead without seeing. She figured Mr. Hartley would probably ask her how she got to be so stupid—how anyone could possibly get so many problems wrong. Maybe he wanted to talk about sending her back to fourth grade. Or maybe he just wanted to yell at her.

Well, all she could do was try to explain. Ms. Austin and her other teachers understood how hard dyslexia made things sometimes. They knew that having a learning disability didn't make Alison stupid, it just made her different. She would just have to get the substitute teacher to understand that, too.

Luckily, Alison didn't have to explain.

"Alison, I was talking to a couple of your other teachers during lunch," Mr. Hartley began.

Mr. Hartley was perched on the edge of Ms. Austin's

big wooden desk at the front of the room.

"Uh huh," Alison said. She grasped the sides of her chair nervously and took a deep breath. "Listen, Mr. Hartley. If this is about that math test, there's something you should probably know about me—"

Mr. Hartley held up one hand to stop her. "There's no need to explain. In fact, I want to apologize to you," he said. "I thought that surprise test would be a good idea. Sometimes students don't pay much attention when there's a substitute teacher, and since Ms. Austin probably won't be back until Monday, I wanted to make sure you kids learned something this week. But as soon as I looked at your test, I suspected that something was going on. I asked around, and your other teachers told me you're dyslexic. I'm sorry I put you through that."

Alison was surprised. The teacher was apologizing to her? "Um, that's okay," she said. "I guess you had no way of knowing." She felt a surge of hope. Maybe Mr. Hartley would throw out that horrible grade. Maybe it wouldn't count at all!

"That's why I want to give you another chance to take my test," Mr. Hartley went on.

Alison's heart sank. There was no way she could ever pass. Not if she took it a million times!

The teacher smiled at the look on her face. "Don't worry," he said. "You won't have to take the exact same test. I studied a lot about learning disabilities in college, and I'm going to write a special word-problem exam tonight just for you. You can take it tomorrow during lunch. Okay?"

"Okay," Alison said a bit hopefully. "Thanks, Mr. Hartley."

A special test sounded a little better, but Alison was still nervous. Word problems were hard for her, that was all there was to it. She wasn't sure she could do much better, even on a special retest. Still, what else could she do but try her best?

After school, Alison walked home with her friends as usual. She told them all about her bad grade and Mr. Hartley's offer.

"That's good," Megan said. "It sounds like he really does understand about dyslexia. I'm sure you'll do much better on the retest."

Alison nodded slowly and kicked at a stone on the sidewalk. It flew into a pile of colorful leaves that someone had just raked off their front lawn. "I guess so," she said. "But what if I don't? What if I do just as badly as I did on the first one?"

"You won't," Keisha assured her, reaching over and giving her a quick hug. "You can do it. You know you can!"

Alison must have still looked uncertain. Rose gave her a searching glance. "Don't let your own nervousness get you

down, Ali," she advised. "My grandfather always likes to tell me that the only thing I really have to fear is fear itself."

Alison thought about that for a second. It made sense, sort of. "But how do you stop yourself from being afraid?" she asked. "I'm usually not scared of anything. I'm not used to it!"

Her friends laughed.

"That's true," Keisha said, her brown eyes sparkling. "Ali is the only one of us who wasn't afraid to jump off the high board at the swimming pool when we were all in first grade, remember?"

"I remember," Megan said. She grinned. "I also remember that she was the first one to volunteer at chorus tryouts. She didn't even seem nervous."

"And what about the time she challenged those high school boys to a snowball fight?" Heather added.

Alison couldn't help smiling as she listened to her friends. They were right—she had done lots of things that most people would consider brave. But to her, those kinds of things didn't seem like such a big deal. Some of them had been scary, but they had been exciting and interesting, too. This kind of fear was different. She just didn't know if she could face it.

"I don't know, guys," Alison replied. "Every time I think about that awful test, my hands start to shake and my heart starts pounding like I just ran a marathon or something. What if I'm so nervous tomorrow that I can't concentrate? I might do even worse than I did today. I might even get a big fat zero this time!"

"Why don't you call your tutor?" Megan suggested.

For a second, Alison felt hopeful. Her reading tutor had helped her in so many ways. Maybe she could give her some tips on tackling this test.

Then she remembered. Her face fell. "I can't," she said. "She's away on vacation this whole week."

Rose gave her a sympathetic look. "How about talking to Ellie, then?" she said. "She was really helpful when I was scared about trying out for the chorus. She had lots of tricks and hints about staying calm and focusing on what I was doing so I didn't have time to get nervous. I know that taking a test isn't exactly like performing in front of a crowd, but—"

Alison didn't even let her finish. "That's a great idea!" she cried. Suddenly she felt better than she had all day. Until recently, Rose had been terrified of singing in front of a group. But after talking to Ellie, she had tried out for the school chorus along with her friends—and made it. If anyone could help Alison with her test fears, it was Ellie. "Come on, let's go see her right now!" she added.

The five girls raced down Primrose Street. Soon they reached Ellie's rambling Victorian house. It was white with blue trim; a picket fence lined the sidewalk, and the leaves on the trees and bushes in the yard had turned beautiful hues of orange, crimson, and gold.

A teenage girl was hurrying up the front walk toward the house as Alison and her friends approached. She was carrying a large portfolio stuffed with sheet music in one hand and a battered violin case in the other. She

climbed Ellie's front porch steps and pressed the doorbell.

"Uh-oh," Heather said. "It looks like Ellie has a music lesson starting now."

Alison was disappointed. It was obvious that Heather was right. "Rats," she muttered. "I guess we shouldn't bother her right now." She sighed. "And I guess I should go home and start studying. I'll call her later."

An hour later Alison dropped her math book on her bed and wandered downstairs to the kitchen for a snack. For once, she had the large, sunny room to herself. Her mother was catering a wedding, and her father was in the living room reading the newspaper. All three of her brothers were out; she didn't know where they were, and she didn't really care. The only thing she cared about was that it had been unusually peaceful and quiet in the house all afternoon. She had gotten a lot of studying done. But she was still feeling anxious about the test. All the studying in the world wouldn't help her if she couldn't understand the questions.

She decided to try calling Ellie. Figuring the violin lesson would be over by now, she went to the kitchen phone and dialed the number.

Ellie sounded happy to hear from her, as usual. Feeling slightly better already, Alison hurriedly explained her problem. "So Rose reminded me about all those tricks you taught her," she said. "You know, to help her calm down and concentrate. I was hoping you could teach them to me. I'm going to need all the help I can get when I take that retest tomorrow."

"Certainly," Ellie said. "I'm sure I can help. A piano student just arrived, but he's my last lesson of the day. Why don't you come over in an hour?"

Chapter

Three

ELLIE'S EMERGENCY

Alison arrived at Ellie's house right on time. She climbed the steps of the wide front porch and pressed the doorbell. The chimes sounded through the house. But two or three minutes passed and nobody came.

Alison noticed a long, white envelope tucked in the frame of the door. Her own name was written on it in Ellie's familiar handwriting.

Alison opened the envelope and pulled out a note.

Dear Alison,

I'm so sorry to miss you. Monty was playing out back and got a nasty thorn in his paw. I couldn't get it out myself, so I decided I'd better run him to the vet. I'm sure we'll be back soon. Why don't you go up to the attic while you wait?

Yours, Ellie

Alison was sorry to hear that Ellie's terrier had hurt himself, but she was sure the vet would take good care of him. She tested the doorknob. It turned easily at her touch and the door swung open. Ellie hadn't locked it.

For a second, Alison thought about going home to wait instead. She could practice doing some more word problems from her math book. But she had already studied so hard that her head felt ready to burst, and she couldn't resist the thought of the attic. An interesting adventure might be just the thing to pass the time until Ellie returned.

Alison let herself into the spacious entry hall. Straight ahead was a small, round table. On top of it was a silver box, its burnished surface gleaming against the polished dark wood of the tabletop. Alison carefully lifted the lid and picked up the fancy, scrolled gold key nestled inside. A shiver of anticipation ran through her as she touched the key.

Moments later, she was at the foot of the stairs leading to the attic. She inserted the key into the brass

lock and turned it. The door swung open,
and she reached for the silk cord attached
to the rosy-shaded overhead light.

Alison looked around. Whenever she
was in the attic, she seemed to
find something different. Where
should she look today? Into the
nooks and cubbyholes of Ellie's tall,
old-fashioned desk? Or into the depths of the heavy old
leather and wood brass-bound trunk?

Alison wandered around the light-filled attic for a few
minutes. She peeked into some of the boxes in one
corner. She checked the piles of glittering jewelry and
accessories in the steamer trunk.

Then she walked across the oriental rug that covered
part of the wooden floor. She passed the trunk and
ducked around the full-length mirror. Behind it was a
huge mahogany wardrobe.

"Let's see what I can find in here today," she murmured,
swinging open the wide double doors.

The wardrobe was stuffed full of all kinds of outfits,
carefully hung on wide wooden hangers. Alison flipped
idly through ballgowns, three-piece suits, and stage
costumes of all kinds. Somehow nothing there caught her
interest. So she opened the trunk and rummaged through
its contents.

Suddenly her fingers touched something that felt very different from the silks and wools of the other outfits. It felt smooth. Kind of squeaky. More like a tent or something other than an article of clothing.

Alison couldn't see what the odd-textured fabric was. She reached down and pulled it out. "A life jacket!" she murmured. "Cool!"

The vest looked sort of like the one she'd once worn canoeing. But this one was red and black with yellow trim, and it zipped down the front instead of buckling. Alison reached back into the trunk and pulled out several more pieces of clothing; a blue short-sleeved shirt, a pair of black bike shorts with a green stripe down the side, and waterproof gloves and sandals.

She put on the entire outfit. The life jacket zipped snugly over her upper body. It felt strange—it was kind of hard to move her arms around as much as she usually could.

She walked around to the front of the mirror.

"I wonder what this outfit is for," she murmured to her own reflection, staring at the rubbery surface of the vest.

"Oh, there you are!" called a voice from behind her.

Alison whirled around. She wasn't in the familiar attic anymore. She was standing on craggy, rocky ground surrounded by tall pine trees. The sound of rushing water came from somewhere nearby; she thought it might be a large river. Crisp, fresh air filled her lungs as she breathed in deeply.

A young woman was climbing over a large boulder. She was tall and athletic-looking, with strong arms and shoulders and close-cropped dark hair.

"Hi," Alison said uncertainly.

"Come on," the young woman called to her cheerfully. "The rafters just arrived. And they're dying to meet their new junior river guide."

Alison nodded and scrambled over the boulder after her. So I'm a junior river guide, she thought. That sounds pretty neat. I wonder what I have to do? She figured it probably had something to do with leading hikes along the river or something like that.

Then Alison remembered the life jacket. It was still kind of hard to move around with it on. Maybe hiking wasn't what was in store for her after all. Hmm, she thought, I guess I'll find out soon enough what I'm supposed to do.

She and the woman emerged into a clearing. A broad, swiftly flowing river was visible just beyond, rushing and tumbling over rocks and fallen logs. About half a dozen boys and girls of various ages were standing next to a large pile of equipment. Alison didn't recognize most of it. But she spotted a cooler and a large picnic basket near the bottom of the pile. Behind the equipment was a huge, bright-red rubber raft.

Alison gasped. White-water rafting! That must be what

the life jacket was for. Could she really be a guide? She had never been rafting before in her life! Still, it had always seemed awfully exciting when she read about it in books or saw it in the movies. She couldn't wait to give it a try.

The woman had already stepped forward to speak to the group. "I found her," she said, gesturing to Alison. "This is Alison. She'll be assisting me as your junior river guide. So you should all listen to her, just like you listen to me."

Alison smiled as the other kids said hello and introduced themselves. This was going to be awesome— not only did she get to go white-water rafting, but she got to be second-in-command!

Chapter Four

RIVER
ADVENTURE

Most of the kids in the group were around Alison's age. One girl with big dark eyes and a sprinkling of freckles across the bridge of her nose looked about nine years old. Two boys who looked about thirteen or fourteen weren't paying much attention to what was going on. They were too busy shoving each other, trying to knock each other into a muddy puddle on the riverbank.

The dark-eyed girl raised her hand. "Emily?" she

called. "Can we all really fit into that one raft?"

The young woman smiled reassuringly. "Don't worry, Clara," she told the girl. She walked over to the rubber boat and patted its side. "A fourteen-foot paddle raft like this one can hold eight people easily and safely. Especially since this is just a day trip. We won't need to weigh it down with all the extra equipment we'd need if we were going to be camping overnight."

Just then one of the teenage boys tripped the other one. The second boy went flying, landing face down in the muddy water of the puddle.

Emily frowned. "Kyle! Patrick!" she said sharply. "Are you paying attention? Alison and I are about to go over some basic rules and instructions. It's very important for you to listen carefully. Every member of the team has to stay alert and ready to act, or we could all be in big trouble. Do you understand?"

"Sure," muttered Patrick. "Sorry."

"Yeah, sorry," added Kyle.

Alison saw the boys rolling their eyes as Emily turned away to address the group again, though Emily didn't seem to notice. Still, after her sharp words the pair quieted down for a while and stopped shoving each other.

"As you know," Emily said, "we'll be rafting today on the Rattlesnake River." She waved a hand at the river rushing past.

"Yeah!" Kyle called out excitedly, pumping his fist in the air. "We're going to run the Rattlesnake!"

"Not exactly," Emily corrected calmly. "A lot of people think of rafting as 'running the river.' But what we'll actually be doing is running small sections of it, taking them one at a time. A bunch of puny people like us is no match for the power of a whole river. But by using our heads and thinking about what we're doing step by step, in small increments, we can handle the trip."

A younger boy raised his hand. "How dangerous is the Rattlesnake River?" he asked. Alison thought he sounded a little bit nervous.

"The section we'll be traveling is what's known as Class Two and Three," Emily replied. "That's on the international scale, which goes from Class One to Class Six. Since a lot of you are beginners, these rapids should be quite challenging without being too dangerous."

Kyle and Patrick had moved forward a little after Emily yelled at them. Now they were standing near Alison, who was at the back of the group next to the raft. "Big deal," she heard one of the boys mutter.

"Sounds like a wimpy baby river," the other one whispered.

The first boy giggled. "It must be a wimpy little river, if they sent a wimpy little junior river guide to help lead us."

Alison's face got red and hot. They were talking about her! She almost turned around to confront them, but forced herself to hold back. She would prove to them that she knew what she was doing once they got out on the river.

Emily was standing farther away, at the front of the group, where she couldn't hear the boys' comments. "Does everyone have a helmet?" she asked. She looked around as each person held up padded headgear.

Alison noticed an extra helmet sitting with the equipment near the boat. The color matched her life preserver, so she figured it was hers. She picked it up and settled it firmly on her head, fastening the strap snugly under her chin.

Emily turned toward her and smiled. "Alison, why don't you talk about our PFDs?"

Alison knew exactly what to say. She nodded and pointed to her life jacket. "PFD stands for 'personal flotation device'," she explained. "That's the official name for a life jacket. It will keep you afloat in case you fall out of the raft."

Kyle or Patrick—Alison still couldn't keep track of which boy was which—snorted loudly. "I don't need one of those," he said. "I know how to swim."

Emily shook her head. "Being able to swim isn't enough," she said sternly. "The river is unpredictable. You could be caught in a strong current, or you could hit your head and be knocked unconscious."

Alison demonstrated the proper way to wear the PFD,

then helped Emily check to make sure that everyone's was on correctly. "It may be a little harder than usual to move your arms around freely," she said. "But it's important to wear your PFD at all times when we're on the water."

"All right, very good," Emily said. "Now we'll show you some of the other equipment we'll have with us in the boat."

Together, she and Alison pointed out the paddles, air pumps, buckets for bailing out the bottom of the boat, emergency signals, cooler and picnic basket full of snacks and fresh water, and some other items. The last thing that Emily held up was a square nylon bag.

"This is a throw bag," she explained. She opened it to reveal a length of rope stuffed inside. "It's one of our most important pieces of rescue equipment. It can be thrown to a person stranded in the water. We'll have two of these throw bags in the raft with us just in case of trouble. As I said, the waters we'll be traveling aren't especially rough. But it always pays to be prepared when you're dealing with nature. It can surprise you."

Next it was time to review a few lessons on maneuvering the raft in the water. Alison soon figured out that the other kids had practiced the basics of paddling before they even came out to the river. She paid close attention as Emily went over everything once again.

"As I explained back at the lodge, our two most basic maneuvers are pivots and ferries," Emily said. "Just about all your other moves will be variations of those two moves. Who can tell me what a pivot is?"

Clara raised her hand. "I think it's like a turn," she said, sounding a little uncertain. "It's when you swivel the raft around to the right or the left."

"That's right," Emily said with a smile. "We can use our paddles to rotate our craft in either direction. That's a pivot. How about a ferry?"

"I know!" Kyle called out without raising his hand. "It's a big boat that carries cars and stuff." He and Patrick started laughing.

"Very funny," Emily said drily. "Anybody else want to give me an answer? A *serious* answer?"

A short, red-haired girl volunteered. "When you ferry, it means you're moving the raft across the river's current," she said.

Emily nodded. "Exactly right," she said. "Before we ferry, we'll usually have to pivot to the correct angle. Then we paddle ourselves in the proper direction, until we're at a new point in the current either to the right or left of our original position."

"You mean we'll have to paddle against the current?" Patrick called out.

Emily frowned. Alison thought she looked slightly annoyed. "Not really, Patrick," she said patiently. "It's like I explained earlier. You can paddle straight upstream, against the current, or downstream with it. But it's not a ferry unless you change position from side to side. Got it?"

Alison nodded along with Patrick. It made perfect sense to her. She couldn't wait to try it.

"One more thing to keep in mind," Emily said. "When I call out a direction, it will be based on the direction and path of the current. And the direction of the current isn't always the same as the direction of the riverbanks. Don't get mixed up and think of them as the same thing."

That one confused Alison for a second. Then she glanced over her shoulder at the river. Even in the relatively calm stretch of it that was visible from where they were, she saw that the water tumbled over itself in all sorts of different directions, sometimes flowing straight down between the widely spaced banks, but just as frequently swirling from side to side like a slithering snake. Then she understood what Emily meant. Their raft

would be carried along by the moving water—the current. Understanding where the current was heading next was much more important than paying attention to the shape of the shoreline.

Emily finished reviewing all the information they would need to know. She also showed them a map of the river, with their route marked clearly on it. It was almost time to get started. "All right, let's have fun, everyone," she concluded. "There's just one more very important thing I want to emphasize. Once we're out on the river, I'm in charge. No questions, no arguing. I'm the captain of our little ship, and all of you are the crew. Our safety— even our lives—could depend on how well you all listen and obey. Got it?"

Everyone nodded, even Kyle and Patrick.

Emily smiled. "Okay," she said. "Let's go!"

Chapter

Five

RUNNING THE RAPIDS

Moments later the raft was in the water, drifting out of the slow-moving eddies near the shore toward the rushing current in the middle of the river. Everyone was on board. Emily had taken her seat in the middle of the back of the raft. Alison was on one side at the front. The dark-eyed girl, Clara, was opposite her.

All the paddlers sat on the seats of a metal frame fitted into the rubber raft. Alison braced her feet against the bottom of the frame to keep herself steady and grasped her paddle firmly in both hands. She couldn't wait to hit their first section of rapids!

The water was fairly calm at the spot where they launched the boat. Emily shouted instructions as the current then grabbed the raft and carried it downstream. Soon the paddlers had figured out how to move the raft where they wanted it to go, to pivot and ferry as a team, following the route Emily had mapped out for them and avoiding unexpected obstacles in the river.

The raft moved swiftly through the water. Waves slapped up against it from time to time, sending chilly showers of spray into the boat and all over the paddlers. Soon Alison's face and hair were drenched.

But she was having a great time so far. She reacted quickly to each of Emily's commands, working her paddle as she'd just learned, helping the others move the boat where it was supposed to go. It was fun to maneuver through the current, pivoting and ferrying to find the best route.

Clara was sitting just across from Alison. She seemed to be having fun, too, although she looked a little nervous. Alison could tell that the younger girl was paying close attention to all the instructions Emily was calling out from the back of the raft. Sometimes it was hard to hear her over the roar of the river and the slapping of the water against the boat. The crew was so busy that there was no time for any talking.

"Okay, everyone!" Emily shouted after a few minutes. "We're just coming to our first section of rapids. Ready? Good—because there's no turning back now!"

Alison glanced forward. Sure enough, she could see a change in the water just ahead. The dark-green surface of the river was becoming more and more broken by spots of frothy, churning water that looked much lighter in color as it tumbled over and around large boulders and jagged rocks.

"Now I see why they call it *white*-water rafting," Clara shouted to Alison.

Alison smiled and nodded. The rapids looked scary, but exciting, too. She wiped some spray out of her eyes, then once again gripped her paddle firmly as she waited for Emily's next instruction.

After that, things seemed to happen very quickly. Her voice firm and commanding, Emily steered her crew around obstacle after obstacle, choosing the best course through the rapids and avoiding potentially dangerous drop-offs, whirlpools, and shallows—as well as the many huge, scary-looking rocks that seemed to come out of nowhere.

Before Alison knew it, it was over. They floated out of

the rapids and found
themselves in another calm
section of the river.

"Whew!" Patrick shouted.
"That was awesome!" He let
go of his paddle with one
hand and high-fived Kyle.

"All right, boys," Emily
called. "I know you're excited. But
don't forget where you are. The river can take you by
surprise if you're not careful, even in a seemingly calm
spot like this."

Kyle was sitting just behind Alison. She heard him
snort. "What a spoilsport," he whispered to Patrick.

Alison frowned. She liked Emily a lot, and she didn't
want to think that the boys were making fun of her. Still,
she couldn't blame Kyle and Patrick too much. Rafting
was a lot of fun. It was hard to remember to be careful *all*
the time.

But Alison was too busy to waste much time thinking
about Kyle and Patrick. Soon the calm water ended, and
the raft once again entered a section of rushing rapids.
Alison was starting to understand what Emily had been
talking about earlier—it really did seem that the river came
along in sections. All the paddlers had to do was handle
each section as they reached it and they would be fine.

They entered another section of rushing, tumbling white water. "This is fun!" Clara called across the boat to Alison.

Alison grinned at the younger girl. "I know!" she shouted back. "Seeing the wilderness this way is a lot more exciting than hiking, isn't it?"

Clara turned to answer. At that moment a large rock seemed to come out of nowhere in the river, rising up in a sea of foam and flying spray just a few feet in front of the boat. Emily shouted out a string of instructions, and all the paddlers went to work immediately to maneuver around the obstacle.

But Alison could see that Clara was in trouble. The younger girl had been caught off-guard, and as she turned to plunge her paddle into the water, a smaller rock popped up on her side of the raft. Clara's paddle struck it hard, Alison could hear the sound it made even over the roaring rapids. Clara was jerked back in her seat by the impact. Her right arm flew back and grappled for a hold, but her left hand clung stubbornly to the paddle's handle. At the same time, the swirling water pulled at the other end of the paddle. Suddenly the boat tipped steeply to the right as it slid over a swell, and Clara started to slip sideways.

"Clara!" Alison cried anxiously. What would happen if the girl fell overboard in this rough current?

"Don't fight the water, Clara!" Emily shouted. "Just drop the paddle if you have to! We have extras."

Before the words were out of her mouth, the boat righted itself and Clara regained her balance. She was still holding the paddle with her left hand. Now she gripped it tightly with her right as well. "I'm okay," she said breathlessly. "I've got it."

"Good," Emily called. "Nice save, Clara. But that just goes to show that it only takes a second for the river to get the upper hand if you don't give it your full attention. We've got to stay alert, people!"

Clara nodded grimly.

Alison could see that the younger girl was shaken up —her face was white, and her eyes were wide and frightened. "It's all right, Clara," she called encouragingly. "You did it. You're fine."

The girl shot her a grateful look. But she still looked kind of scared. Alison didn't blame her. It had been a close call.

After the third set of rapids ended, the river drifted lazily around a wide, gentle bend. The crew didn't have to do much paddling. They just let the current pull the boat downstream.

"Okay, take a breather if you can, everyone," Emily called out. The water was so much calmer that she hardly even had to shout to make herself heard. "We'll be coming to a couple of rough spots just around the bend, so you'll need to be ready."

"I hope the rough spots you're talking about are more exciting than that last set of rapids. They were easy," Kyle bragged. "I could have paddled through them with my eyes closed."

"Me, too," Patrick put in loudly. "I get bigger rapids than that in my bathtub."

Both boys started laughing.

"Enough!" Emily said, sounding annoyed. "There's no time for joking around. Like I said, as soon as we get around the next bend, we'll—"

Patrick cut her off. "Next time, I'm going rafting over Niagara Falls," he shouted jokingly. "That's what I call *real* white water!"

Alison was starting to feel annoyed herself. They were supposed to be paying attention, not goofing around. Hadn't Kyle and Patrick learned anything from Clara's close call? She was thinking about turning around and saying something to the boys. After all, she was the second-in-command.

But before she could open her mouth, she saw Clara spin around on her seat. The younger girl's face was white. "Be quiet!" Alison cried at the two boys. "Stop goofing around, or you'll put us all in danger!"

The boys stared at her in surprise for a second. Then

MARY A. WHITE SCHOOL
Library Media Center
Grand Haven, MI 49417

they started to laugh again.

"Oh, boo-hoo!" Kyle exclaimed. "I'm so scared."

"Me, too!" Patrick added. "Boo-hoo! I might fall in!"

Alison noticed that it was getting harder to hear them. There was an increasing rush and roar from somewhere just ahead. The raft was approaching another curve in the river, and she couldn't see the water beyond. The boat seemed to be picking up speed once again.

Clara was still twisted around, looking at the boys.

"Quiet — now!" Emily barked sharply from the back. "Clara, turn around. We're almost there."

Clara spun around quickly, looking frightened. Just then the raft hit a wave and jerked to the side. The girl lost her balance and fell off her seat as the force of the water flung her halfway over the thick, rounded side of the raft.

"Help!" she shrieked in terror, her arms flailing uselessly. This time there was no way she could hold on to her paddle. It flew far out into the river and was quickly sucked beneath the churning, swirling surface. The raft had just spun around the last bit of the bend, faster than Alison would have thought possible, and entered a wide, wild section of rapids, much rougher than any they had tackled so far.

Alison reacted quickly as Clara slid farther over the side. She reached across and grabbed the back of the

girl's life jacket, hauling her back into the raft. She didn't
let go until she saw Clara catch hold of the inner frame.

"Nice work, Alison!" Emily shouted above the roaring
rapids. "Quick, everyone! Left pivot—now!"

Alison immediately went to work. But behind her,
something was wrong.

"Boys!" Emily yelled. "Snap out of it! Come on!"

Alison kept paddling, but she glanced over her
shoulder at the rest of the crew. Most of the others were
doing as Emily said. But Kyle and Patrick were gaping at
Clara, their faces pale and their paddles held up out of

the water. At the same time, Emily was trying to paddle with one hand while passing a spare paddle forward for the girl.

"Boys!" Emily shouted once more. She waited until Clara had a firm hold of the paddle. Then she leaned forward in the lurching, plunging raft to poke Patrick in the shoulder.

That woke him up, and he started to paddle. So did Kyle.

But as Emily leaned back into her seat, the raft suddenly hit a deep hole in the rapids, sending the boat jerking sharply downward.

Alison watched in horror. Emily's arms flew up, and her hands windmilled desperately as she tried to keep her balance.

It didn't do any good. She flew over the side of the raft into the rushing current!

Chapter Six

A DANGEROUS RESCUE

Alison gasped as she saw Emily tumble through the rapids alongside the boat. A wild current grabbed the woman and swiftly carried her forward, until she was almost ten yards ahead of them. Alison heard the others screaming and yelling in panic behind her.

Alison felt like panicking, too. Their leader was in the water; her life jacket was keeping her afloat, but she was in constant danger of smashing against a rock or getting trapped in a deadly whirlpool.

Besides that, the raft was quickly going out of control. It skidded around until the current was carrying it along sideways. Each wave and hole smacked into its taut rubber exterior, threatening to upset it and send everyone into the tumbling rapids. It was hard to see anything through the thick spray, or to hear anything over the wild roar of the river.

I'm the junior river guide, Alison told herself. I'm in charge now. She had to save the raft—and Emily.

She quickly decided to make everyone paddle straight after Emily. They had to catch up to her and haul her aboard somehow, without crashing into a rock while they were doing it—like the huge, craggy one looming just a dozen yards ahead . . .

Alison forced herself to take a deep breath. She had to calm down. The only advantage she had over the river was her brain, and if she didn't use it, they were all doomed. She forced herself to pause and take a second to study the rapids just ahead. She had to think, to figure out the best way to proceed.

Once she concentrated, Alison saw almost immediately what they had to do. "Pivot left when I count three," she shouted over her shoulder at the paddlers behind her.

"Are you crazy?" Patrick yelled back. "We've got to go to the right around that rock. Otherwise we'll be going away from Emily."

Alison gritted her teeth. She knew that Patrick was wrong—dead wrong. If they followed Emily to the right of the rock, they might never catch up to her. She was too far ahead of them already. Besides, the rapids to the right were filled with dozens of small, jagged rocks, turning the water into a wide swath of pure foam. Alison could see that the current flowed more swiftly, as well as more smoothly, on the left. If they could get over that way, they might be able to reach Emily and toss her a line.

But there wasn't enough time to explain that to the others. They would be at the big rock in a matter of seconds. "Quiet, everyone!" Alison yelled at the top of her lungs. "I'm the captain. Do as I say. One, two, three, go!"

For a second she was afraid that the boys wouldn't obey her. But they did. The raft pivoted perfectly, taking them safely around the rock and into the swiftly running current to their left.

"Kyle! Grab one of those throw bags," Alison called over her shoulder, keeping her eyes trained on Emily's brightly colored helmet as it bobbed through the water just ahead. It was impossible for her to tell if Emily was conscious and swimming, or just floating

RESCUE BAG

along limply. She felt like crossing her fingers for good luck. But there was no time.

"Huh?" Kyle replied. "Grab what?"

Alison realized that he had no idea what she was talking about. He must not have been paying attention to that part of the lecture.

Luckily, Clara had. She stretched back, keeping a tight hold on the raft, and grabbed one of the throw bags from where Emily had stowed it. "Here you go, Alison," she cried.

Alison took the bag without looking at it. Something new was happening up ahead. Emily had just grabbed onto a tall, jagged rock in her path and was clinging to it. Alison felt like laughing with relief. She was awake! She was alive!

But they were all still in big trouble.

"Quick, everyone!" Alison yelled as she got the throw bag ready. "Pivot and ferry. We've got to get to the shallows along the shore!" The water near the riverbank was almost still. If they could get there, they could slow down or even stop long enough to toss the line to Emily.

This time no one argued or hesitated. The whole crew threw themselves into their paddling. Soon they were out of the rushing current and into the gently flowing area just a few feet from shore. The bank was too steep and overgrown for them to pull up. And even though the current was much slower there, it hadn't stopped entirely.

It was going to be impossible to stay in one spot for more than a few seconds. That would make it hard to throw the bag accurately. Alison decided she would just have to do her best.

She paused again, checking out the situation carefully. When she was sure she understood what she had to do, she spoke to her crew again.

"Okay, we're almost even with Emily," she called. "Pivot right, and keep it as steady as you can. I'm going to toss the throw bag."

The crew obeyed once again. Alison forced herself to wait until the raft had reached the spot she had chosen. Then she took a deep breath, and threw the bag toward Emily, letting the line snake out as the bag flew across the water.

All of Alison's years playing softball and tennis really paid off. Her aim was strong and accurate. The bag landed just a few feet upstream from the rock to which Emily was clinging. The current grabbed it and rushed downstream with it, but Emily loosened her grip with one hand and grabbed it as it floated past.

"Great throw, Alison!" someone shouted from the back of the raft.

"Thanks," Alison answered to no one in particular. "Now, quiet. We've still got to bring her in. Get ready to pivot right again."

It wasn't easy, but Alison managed to direct the raft and help pull Emily in at the same time. By the time the guide was alongside, the rough riverbanks had given way to a rocky but flat section of shoreline. At Alison's direction, the crew beached the raft and then helped Emily ashore.

Once she had recovered her breath, Emily turned to Alison with a grateful smile. "Thanks," she said. "I was pretty worried there for a while. Those rapids were rough— they felt a lot closer to Class Three than Class Two to me. You did a great job. You didn't act like a junior river guide out there. You acted like a real leader."

"Thank you," Alison said. She was exhausted, but exhilarated, too. She had done it! She had really done it!

"No, thank *you*," Emily said, clapping Alison on the shoulder. "There's no question about it. The river just gave you more training than anything I could dream up, and you passed its test with flying colors. You're definitely ready to be an *official* junior river guide. Congratulations!"

Chapter

Seven

CAMPFIRE CONVERSATION

Alison was so excited by what Emily had said that she hardly even felt tired anymore. That was a good thing—after a brief rest, Emily asked the other rafters to help her push the boat back into the river again so they could continue on their way. Some of them were nervous about going on with the trip after the incident, but Emily quickly reassured them.

"We've got to keep going," she said firmly. "There's no other good way out of here except down the river.

Besides, you shouldn't feel upset or worried about what happened. You should feel good—all of you. Something unexpected happened, but you handled it and made sure it turned out all right. You all worked as a team, you all followed your leader, Alison, and everybody came through it just fine. Right?"

"Right!" said one little boy loudly. He stood up and saluted like a soldier. That made everyone laugh, and after that the whole group seemed to relax a little. They made sure all the supplies in the raft were secure and got ready to hit the water again.

The rest of the trip was exciting but safe. The crew rode several other sets of rapids. Nobody else fell in, and there were no other mishaps. Alison was sure she'd never had so much fun in her life. She loved white-water rafting!

All too soon, the group reached the end of the trip. Emily guided them out of the rushing current into a wide, calm section of river and toward a gently sloping beach covered with tiny stones and moss. Other guides were waiting to help pull the raft ashore and unload it, and Alison happily unstrapped her helmet and dropped it on a pile with the others. She peeled off her gloves, tucked them in the waistband of her shorts, and stretched her arms above her head. Her muscles were a little sore, but in a way that felt good.

It was almost dusk, and Alison could see a large, crackling fire several yards back from the beach. She headed toward it, and the sharp smell of burning wood met her nose—along with the very welcome smell of cooking food. Suddenly she realized that she was ravenously hungry.

"Cool!" one of the other rafters yelled. "Dinner!"

"I'm starving," someone else added.

Before long the whole group had gathered around the roaring campfire, to dry off, warm up, and eat the delicious food that the waiting guides had cooked for them. There were hot dogs, hamburgers, chicken legs, and corn on the cob. Foil-wrapped potatoes were roasting in the embers at the edge of the fire. Emily took snacks out of the picnic basket and set them out. Sections of logs scattered in a wide circle around the fire pit served as seats for the hungry crew.

Alison grabbed a well-done burger off the platter and found a spot next to Clara. "Mmm, this smells delicious," she said contentedly. She took a big bite. The burger tasted just as good as it smelled.

Clara smiled shyly. "I was hoping I'd get a chance to talk to you, Alison," she said, setting her own hot dog down on her paper plate. "I wanted to tell you I had a

really great time today. And to thank you for an adventure I'll never forget—you really showed me what teamwork is all about."

"Thanks, Clara," Alison said. The girl's words made her feel bashful. After all, she had only done what had to be done. Still, she was proud that she had been able to come through. And it was all because she had listened and learned from Emily—and realized that even in an emergency, immediate action wasn't as important as keeping a cool head and figuring out the best way to proceed. "I couldn't have done it without you guys, though," Alison added.

Clara shrugged and laughed. "I guess not," she said. "But you seemed so calm and in control the whole time. You made me feel less scared. I think I'll be much braver next time I go rafting. And I'll probably have even more fun."

"Great," Alison said. "You mean you're going to do this again someday?"

"Someday soon, I hope," Clara confirmed. That shy smile crossed her face again, and her wide, dark eyes danced. "Who knows? Maybe someday I'll even get to be a junior river guide myself."

"I bet you will," Alison said, grinning back. She meant it, too.

The two girls chatted about the trip for a few more minutes. Then Clara finished her hot dog and got up to get another. A second later Alison heard someone clear his throat behind her.

She turned and saw Patrick and Kyle standing there with burgers in their hands and sheepish expressions on their faces.

"Uh, hi, Alison," Kyle said. "We have something to say."

"What is it?" Alison asked cautiously. She hoped they weren't there to make fun of her again. She was feeling really good, and she didn't want anything to ruin it—especially a couple of goof-off boys.

Patrick looked embarrassed. He stared at his feet. "We wanted to apologize," he mumbled. "For not paying attention and all."

Kyle nodded and shrugged. "Right," he said. "We're sorry we gave you a hard time."

"It's okay." Alison could hardly believe her ears. It made her good mood even better. "Just be sure to remember that if you two ever go white-water rafting again," she told them.

"We will," Patrick assured her quickly. "But if we go again, we might try an easier river. You know, Class One instead of Class Two."

"Yeah," Kyle added with a grin. "Or maybe Class Negative One. Also known as my bathtub."

The two boys laughed. This time Alison laughed with them. She waved as they stuffed their burgers into their mouths and wandered away. And she rolled her eyes and shook her head when Kyle pushed Patrick into a shrub and Patrick shoved Kyle into one of the guides. Boys!

Alison stood up and looked over the campsite. All around her, people were eating and talking, resting and enjoying a relaxing evening after their action-packed day. It was a happy, peaceful scene, and Alison wished she could stay longer and enjoy it. But it was getting late, and she knew it was time for her to be going. There was just one problem. Where was she going to find a mirror out in the wilderness?

Suddenly she remembered. She hurried toward the beached raft. Most of the equipment was still in it. She found the emergency kit. It was full of items meant to help rafters signal for help if they were stranded. It contained a whistle, some flares—and a mirror to flash a sunlight signal at a helicopter or other rescue party. It was small, but it would do.

"So long, Rattlesnake River," Alison whispered, moving behind a clump of thick underbrush. "It's been fun."

Chapter

Eight

THE RETEST

Alison blinked. The sunlight pouring through the windows of Ellie's attic seemed very bright after the dim light of the campfire. She quickly changed into her regular clothes.

She let herself out of the attic, clattered down the stairs and locked the door carefully behind her.

"Alison?" Ellie's voice called from the kitchen at the back of the house. "Is that you, dear?"

"It's me," Alison called back cheerfully. She waited in

the hallway until Ellie joined her. "I didn't know you were home. How's Monty?"

"I just got here a moment ago," Ellie said. Just then, the little terrier bounded into the hall after her, barking happily at Alison. He had a small white bandage on one paw, but seemed as friendly and cheerful as always. "And Monty's fine, as you can see," Ellie added.

Alison bent down to hug the dog. Monty panted and licked her nose eagerly. "Great," Alison said with a giggle. "Well, I guess I'd better get going."

"What?" Ellie looked surprised. "I thought you wanted to talk about tips for your test tomorrow."

"I did," Alison said. "But now I don't think I need that stuff anymore. I figured out some tips of my own."

Ellie's surprised expression changed to a smile. "Ah," she said. "I see." She walked over to the little silver box and held it open as Alison dropped the key inside. "I'm glad to hear it."

"Me, too," Alison said. "See you later. And thanks!"

The next day Alison hurried to Ms. Austin's room after

lunch. Mr. Hartley was waiting for her.

"All ready?" he asked.

Alison nodded. She felt a flutter in her stomach as the teacher handed her a few sheets of paper, but she forced herself to stay calm.

"I'm ready," she said.

And she was, too. If she kept her cool and remembered everything that her reading tutor had taught her, she could handle this test. She was sure of it.

She picked up her pencil and got started.

Alison was still writing when Mr. Hartley announced that her time was up. But this time she was writing the answer to the last question.

"I'm done," she said, finishing quickly and setting down her pencil. "When are you going to mark it?"

Mr. Hartley chuckled at her eagerness. "Well, we still have a few minutes before the rest of the class returns from lunch," he said. "So I can do it right now if you like."

Alison did her best to sit quietly and not fidget too much as the teacher sat down at his desk and went over her paper. Even though the test was over, she still felt a little bit nervous. But she also felt good. She had understood all of the questions, and that was more than half the battle.

Finally Mr. Hartley leaned back in his chair and looked up. "Well, well," he said, his face neutral.

Alison felt a pang of fear. She *thought* she'd done pretty well. But maybe she was wrong. Had she done just as badly this time? Had she—gulp—done even *worse*?

Then Mr. Hartley's face broke into a broad smile. "Congratulations, Alison," he said. He held up the test paper. "You got a ninety-two. That's an A."

"An A!" Alison cried, hardly daring to believe it. She jumped up and hurried to the teacher's desk to see for herself. "I actually got an A?"

"You sure did," Mr. Hartley said. "I suspected you could do it."

"So did I," Alison said. She paused and grinned. "No, actually, that's not true. I *knew* I could do it!"

Diary

Dear Diary,

It's been days and days now, but I can still hardly believe I got an A on that word problem test! My parents were excited, too, and so was my tutor. Even Ms. Austin was impressed when she came back to school on Monday. (She's fine, by the way. She just had the flu.)

My friends were really envious when I told them about my latest attic adventure. None of them has ever been white-water rafting. Heather is already busy planning a rafting vacation for all of us. Now all we have to do is convince our parents to let us go!

Anyway, if we all make it out on the river someday, I'll know exactly what to do: keep my cool, no matter what happens! (And listen to the guide, of course.) I understand now that fear is sometimes the thing that can scare you the most, and that if you can get past the fear, you can deal with the problem. Does that make sense? Someone a long time ago said it better than me. I asked Rose's grandfather about that quote Rose was talking about. He wrote it down for me, and I taped it to the mirror in my bedroom so I wouldn't forget it. It's "The only thing we have to fear is fear itself." President Franklin Delano Roosevelt said it during his first inaugural address. That was way back in 1933, but his words definitely still make sense today.

Well, I've got to go—confidence alone isn't enough to succeed in math. (President Roosevelt didn't say that, Ms. Austin did.) If I want to keep getting A's on my tests, I've got to study, too. I'd better get started now!

Love, Me *Alison*

MARY A. WHITE SCHOOL
Library Media Center
Grand Haven, MI 49417